DrRoach

First published in Great Britain in 2012 by Boxer Books Limited.

www.boxerbooks.com

Based on an original idea by Sam Williams.

Monstrous Stories™ concept, names, stories, designs and logos
© Boxer Books Limited

Written by Paul Harrison
Paul Harrison asserts his moral right to be identified
as the author of this work.
Text copyright © 2012 Boxer Books Limited

Illustrated by Tom Knight
Tom Knight asserts his moral right to be identified
as the illustrator of this work.
Illustrations copyright © 2012 Tom Knight

The illustrations were prepared using brush, ink and digital.
The text is set in Blackmoor Plain and Adobe Caslon.

ISBN 978-1-907967-33-7
1 3 5 7 9 10 8 6 4 2

Printed in Great Britain

All of our papers are sourced from
managed forests and renewable resources.

Dr Roach's
Monstrous
STORIES

Dr Roach presents

NIGHT OF THE
ZOMBIE
GOLDFISH

a Boxer Books production

Contents

Dr Roach welcomes YOU!

Hello, my favourite little friend! So nice that you could join me. Do you have goldfish? Such ordinary little creatures – and quite boring really. Imagine how much more exciting they would be if they were huge and had legs. Now that would make them more interesting pets, don't you think?

Let's meet Judd Crank and his friend Zak. Two ordinary boys, in an ordinary town, with some very ordinary goldfish.

Who would have thought that those little goldfish would become great monsters and step right out of their tank and into town – looking for trouble.

How, you ask? Come closer, my friend, and I'll tell you all about it.

Welcome to Dr Roach's Monstrous Stories. Enjoy!

Chapter 1
Erupto-Fizz

KABBOOOOFFFF!

Judd Crank peered at the results of his latest experiment through a cloud of thick, purple smoke. Things hadn't gone exactly as planned.

"Hmm, perhaps just the one spoonful of pepper next time," Judd muttered to himself.

Judd loved chemistry. He loved the powders and potions and beakers and tubes. He loved it all so much he had managed to get his mum and dad to let him make a laboratory in the garage. Judd would spend hours there mixing, dabbling and experimenting.

Judd kept a large tank full of
goldfish next to his workbench. Judd
loved his fish as much as he loved
chemistry. He liked their colour and
the feeling of calm they gave him.
He could watch his fish for hours.

He wasn't thinking of his fish right then, though. He was thinking about how to make his experiment, Erupto-fizz, work properly. But what he should have been thinking about was getting ready.

"Judd, are you ready yet?" his mother shouted from the house.

Judd took off his safety glasses, revealing two white circles in the purple soot around his panic-filled eyes. Was he ready yet? Ready for what? Suddenly, he remembered! He was going to Grandma's!

"Erm, yep, nearly Mum. I'm just getting my stuff together," he fibbed.

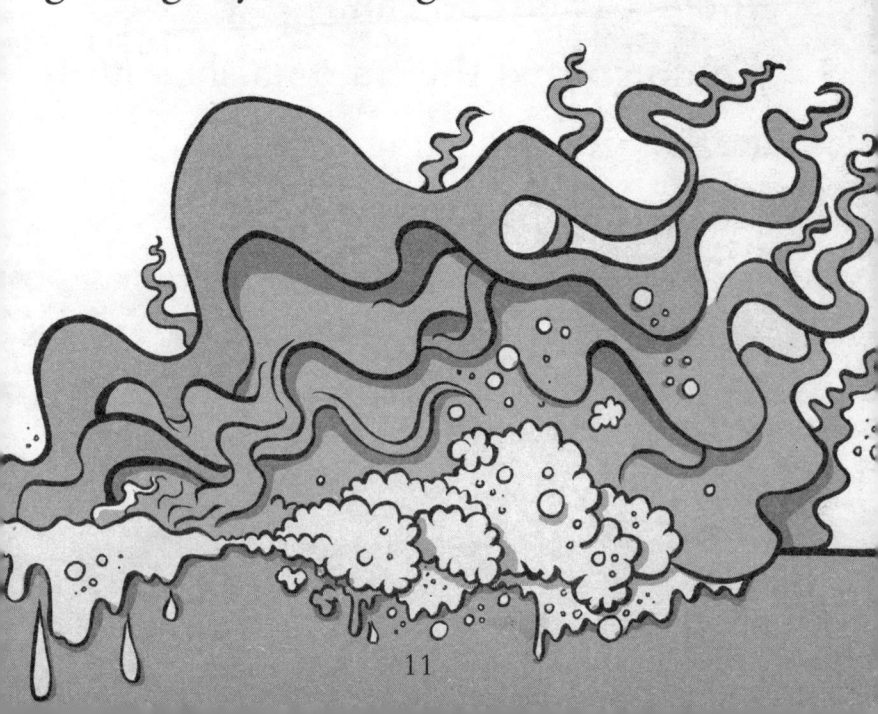

"Judd, we're waiting for you. I hope you're not experimenting in there?"

Quickly, Judd scraped together the remains of the experiment and emptied them into the first empty container he could find – a fish food can.

Judd stuffed the tin on a shelf and dashed out the garage.

"Coming Mum!"

Chapter 2
Fishy fishy flakes

Zak Pietersen was Judd's next door neighbour and most trusted friend. He was the only person Judd would allow to look after his fish. Zak took his fish-feeding duties very seriously and as usual arrived nice and early the next day as he knew finding the fish food could take a while.

Judd's laboratory was always a mess, and today was no different. If anything, it was worse. It looked as if a giant bear had broken in and pulled the place apart to find something tasty to eat. Zak sighed, but then he saw it. Right there on the shelf was a can of:

SOMETHING FISHY FISH FLAKES
–The favourite food of fish.

"Nice one, Judd," he thought.
Happily, Zak unscrewed the lid
and tapped out some of the contents
into the tank and then went over to
Judd's workbench to look at Judd's
latest experiment. Zak could never
make head nor tail of what Judd was
doing, but it all looked very exciting.

BURP!

"Excuse you," said Zak to the person who had belched. Then Zak realised – there *was* no one else!

BURP!

Zak span round in a panic – who was making that noise?

BURP! It was the fish

tank! It looked like a shaken fizzy

drink. Huge bubbles of gas shot to the surface of the water and then exploded in belches, spreading clouds of purple smoke billowing across the laboratory.

In a panic, Zak checked the label on the tin. There it was, clear as day: *Something Fishy Fish Flakes – The favourite food of fish*. It had to be the fish food, hadn't it?

The water inside the fish tank
began to change colour. It went
green, bright red, electric blue,
yellow, and then purple.

FIZZZZZZZZZZ!

WHIZZ! BANG!

Sparks began to shoot into the air, slopping the water all over the floor. The purple smoke swirled thicker and thicker over the edges of the tank, changing colour with the water below.

Zak turned on his heels and ran for it.

Chapter 3
Zombie Goldfish

Zak thought that he had killed Judd's fish, but this wasn't true. The good news was that the fish were still alive. The bad news – no, sorry – the very bad news was that the chemicals Zak had tipped into the tank were actually changing Judd's beautiful, peaceful pets into ...

ZOMBIE GOLDFISH!

There are three things you need to know about zombie goldfish:

1. They are really stupid.

2. Being zombies, they can live on land and walk on their flippers.

3. They are BIG.

As night fell, the goldfish crawled
out of the purple, smoke-covered
water of the tank, slowly clambering
on top of each other like a big,
slippery, fishy pyramid.

They slid over the edge of the tank and onto the garage floor, where they lay getting bigger and bigger. Finally, they hauled themselves upright, shuffled to the door – and broke their way through.

They were heading for town,
and they were

HUNGRY!

Chapter 4
The Happy Haddock

Carp Creek, the town where Judd and Zak lived, was as quiet and sleepy a town as a quiet and sleepy town could ever be – until now.

The zombie goldfish were coming
to town.

The Happy Haddock was Carp
Creek's only restaurant. People wore
their nicest clothes and everyone was
on their best behaviour. It was the
last place you would expect
to see a line of giant goldfish
waddling through
the door.

The head waiter, who obviously needed better glasses, approached the zombies.

"I'm sorry," he said, "I'm afraid I can't allow you in without a tie."

The zombie at the front looked at the waiter for a moment with his big fishy eyes and then tried stuffing the waiter's head into his mouth.

"Euurrrgghhh!" cried the disgusted waiter as he pulled away. "Slimy!"

Fish was no longer on the menu at the Happy Haddock –
the customers were!

The zombie goldfish attacked anything and everything to see if it was food. They nibbled napkins, chomped on chairs, gnawed people's knees and bit their bottoms. Customers and waiters shrieked and screamed and stampeded for the door.

The word was out – the zombie goldfish were in town.

Next it was Carp Creek's fishing store, Hook, Line and Sinker, that got a visit from the gruesome goldfish. The unfortunate customers discovered that the hunters had

become the hunted, as the fish chased the fishermen. Rods, reels and fishing lines went clattering to the floor as the fear-ridden fishermen escaped out the back door.

The townspeople began to panic!

Chapter 5
Return to Carp Creek

When Judd and his parents returned to Carp Creek, they soon discovered that something very fishy was happening. There was a police roadblock and some odd stories of

giant fish. There were more nasty surprises for Judd at home, too.

"My goldfish are gone!" cried Judd, dashing out of the laboratory.

"Perhaps they got fed up with the mess and left," his dad joked.

"No – the door's been broken down, and there's water all over the floor!"

"Honey, no one in Carp Creek would have stolen your fish," his mum reassured him. "Zak will know what happened."

Judd dashed straight to Zak's. He thought about the strange stories of giant fish he'd been hearing. There was no way the two could be connected, right?

"Hi Mrs Pietersen," said Judd as Zak's mum opened the door. "Is Zak home?"

"Sure, he's out back," she replied.

Judd sped past her and into the backyard. There was no one there.

"Zak!" Judd called.

There was no reply.

Then Judd heard a creaking sound from Zak's tree house. Judd looked up – just in time to see Zak duck away from the window.

Puzzled, Judd climbed the ladder to the tree house. Zak was there looking guilty.

"Sorry for killing your goldfish," said Zak quickly.

"You killed them?" said Judd.

"Yeah – I put the food in and the water went all bubbly and purple. Sorry."

"The food under the counter
turned the water bubbly and purple?"
said Judd.

"No, the food on the shelf next
to the tank," Zak replied.

"Next to the tank … oh!" Judd
realised what Zak had done. He'd put
the remains of Judd's last experiment
into the tank. "That wasn't food.
That was my latest experiment –
Erupto-fizz!"

Judd explained to Zak what had happened – but it still didn't explain why there were no goldfish floating in the water.

Unless …
"That's it! Those giant fish –
they're mine!"
"What are you talking about?"
said Zak.

"The powder must have changed them! And it's up to us to change them back!"

Judd jumped up.

"Where are you going?" asked Zak.

"To the lab to make the antidote. C'mon, I'm going to need your help."

Chapter 6
The Trap

The boys raced straight to Judd's laboratory.

"So if you're making the antidote, what do I do?" Zak asked.

"I'm going to need you to attract the fish."

"Attract the fish?"
Zak repeated.

"You're going to lead them into our trap."

"We've got a trap?" asked Zak.

"Not yet – but we will."

Judd started pulling paper, pens and wire out from some boxes in one corner of the garage.

"Here we are," said Judd.

"We're going to trap them with stationery?" asked Zak.

"No, it's your costume," Judd replied. "You need to put it on to lure the fish."

"No way!" said Zak. "Not a chance! No, no, nopey no."

Ten minutes later, Zak was dressed as a large can of Something Fishy Fish Flakes – The favourite food of fish.

"I look ridiculous," Zak grumbled as Judd helped him into the costume.

"You look great – anyway, it's all part of the plan," said Judd. "They're hungry, so they'll follow you."

"They're going to eat me?" Zak exclaimed.

"Not if you're quick," replied Judd cheerfully. "Now go find my fish; I've got chemistry to do. I'll ring your mobile phone when I'm done."

Zak tripped over in his costume for the twentieth time and lay on the ground complaining.

"This is a dumb idea,"

he grumbled. "I wish I *had* killed his dumb fish. How am I supposed to run dressed as a giant can of fish food? And where am I supposed to find those stupid fish anyway?"

Zak struggled to his feet and turned to go home.

There, standing staring at him with big, dead eyes, were fifteen zombie goldfish.

"Oh," said Zak. "There they are."

Chapter 7
The Chase

"Aaaaaaaaaaaaaaaaaaaaaaaaaaaaaaa arrrrrrrrrrrrrggggghhhhhh!" Zak screamed. He was running down the street as fast as his feet could carry him. Unfortunately, this wasn't quite fast enough. Zak's costume stopped him from taking big steps, so the

zombie goldfish were right behind him – and gaining, fast!

BIDDLY-DEE BIDDLY-DOO, BIDDLY-DEE BIDDLY-DOO, WOOP-WOOP, BIDDLY-DEE BIDDLY-DOO

Zak fumbled with the costume and brought out his mobile phone.

BIDDLY-DEE BIDDLY-DOO, WOOP-WOO ...

"Hi," gasped Zak. "Sorry, but this really isn't a great time ..."

"Zak, it's me, Judd – don't hang up!" said the voice on the phone. "Have you found the fish yet?"

"Well, they kind of found me,"
Zak replied.

"Great. Can you get them to
follow you?" asked Judd.

"Oh yeah," said Zak. "That part
of the plan is going too well,
if anything."

Behind him, the zombie goldfish
were getting closer.

"Great," said Judd. "Are you running? You sound out of breath. Never mind. Bring the fish to the swimming pool – I'll be waiting there."

"Can't you come to me?" pleaded Zak, but Judd had already hung up.

The zombies were so close that Zak could almost feel their fishy breath; but Carp Creek's outdoor pool was just around the corner. Behind him, Zak could hear the **SLAP SLAP SLAP** of the zombies' tail fins as they pounded the street.

Zak barged through the entry gates with the goldfish in hot pursuit.

"Judd!" Zak called, looking wildly from side to side as he ran, but it was difficult to see through the narrow eye-slits of his costume. Suddenly, the floor started to feel bouncy. Zak looked down – he was

standing at the end of the diving
board, wobbling over the water.
Carefully, he turned around to get
off, but there, shuffling along the
board towards him, were the zombie
goldfish!

Chapter 8
Celebration Time

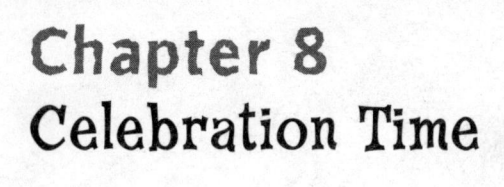

"Zak – jump!"

It was Judd, standing by the edge of the pool. Zak didn't think twice. Splash!

The zombies shuffled to the end
of the board. With fifteen more
splashes, they followed Zak into
the pool. By then Judd was already
fishing Zak out the water.

Zak sat on the side coughing and
spluttering inside his soggy costume.
Judd emptied a large bucket full of
his antidote into
the pool.

Nothing happened. Then …

BURP!

The water began to steam and boil. Great bubbles began to rise and belch green clouds of smoke. The water changed colour from purple, to yellow, to electric blue, to bright red, and then green. The belching got louder and the smoke got thicker, until neither Judd nor Zak could see. Suddenly, there was a massive, final
BUUURRRRPPPPP!
and the boys were showered with a watery green slime.

Eventually, the smoke cleared. Most
of the water that had been in the
swimming pool was now out of the
pool. But there, happily swimming
around in the small amount of water
that was left, were fifteen perfectly
normal-looking goldfish.

"We've done it!" cried Judd.

Zak did not reply. He had fainted.

There was, of course, a big celebration in Carp Creek. The mayor made a long speech, the town band played some terrible music and the local paper took some bad photographs. While the crowd applauded, Judd leaned over to Zak.

"Cheer up, you're a hero," he said.

"Oh sure. You did all the clever stuff. I just dressed up as fish food and got chased

across town by
giant goldfish.
Some hero,"
Zak replied.

"Yeah, but if
you hadn't done
that, I wouldn't have been able to
make the antidote. We're a team."

Zak smiled.

"Yeah, I guess
so. Only one
thing: don't
ever ask me
to feed your
goldfish
again."

Judd
laughed.

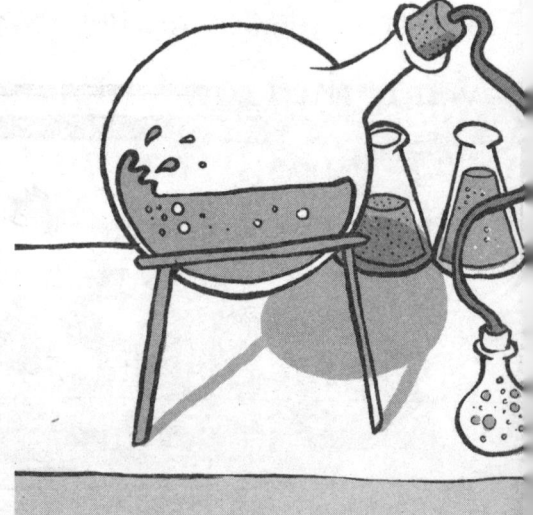

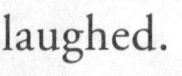

"Seriously though, what are the chances of that ever happening again?"

Across town, in Judd's laboratory, all was quiet – messy, but quiet. In a tank swam fifteen happy, normal goldfish. Normal, that is, apart from the wings that they were beginning to sprout from their backs ...

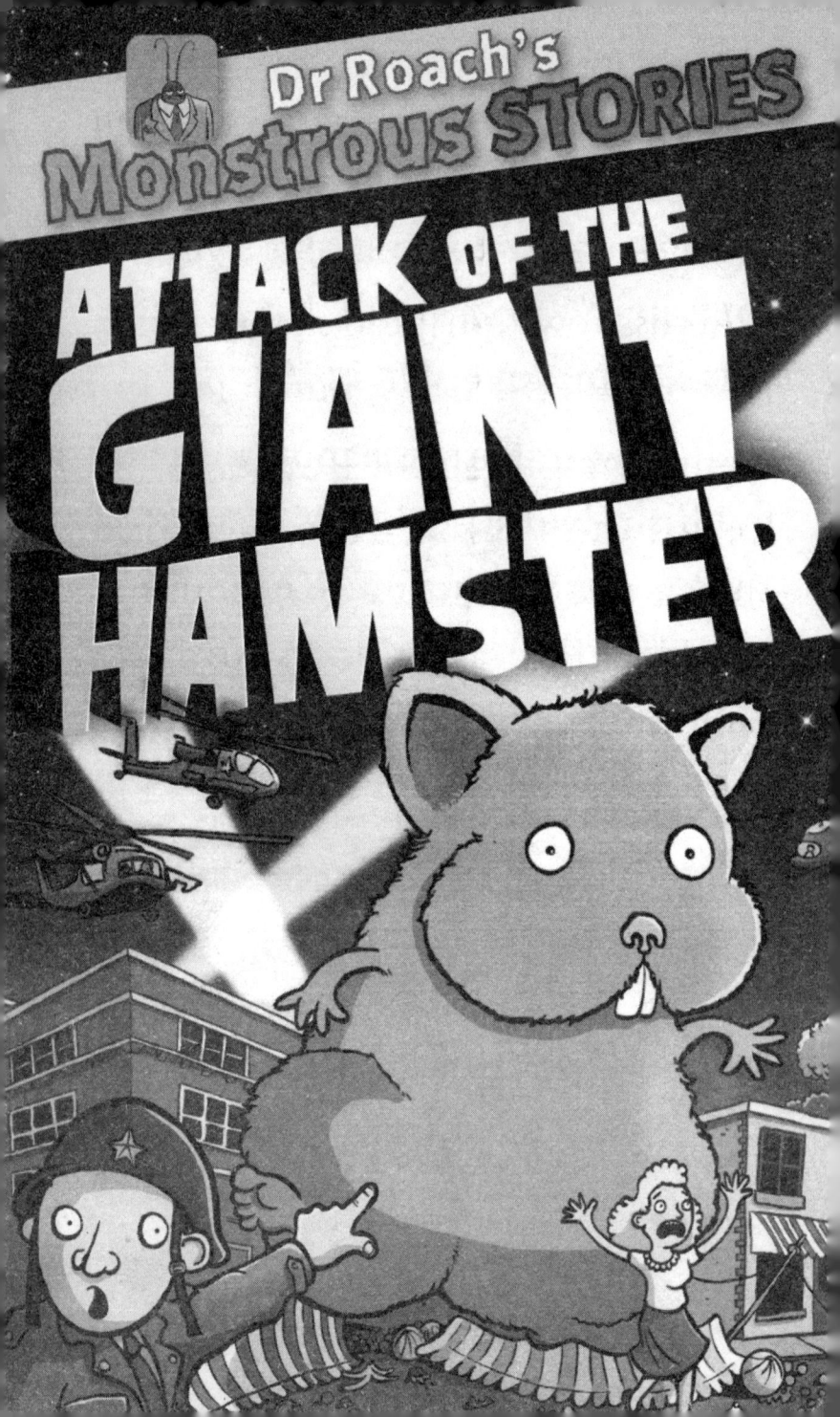

Have you seen those ads that say they will make you beautiful, slim, give you big muscles and even more hair? Pish-posh, I say - it's all make-believe. Or is it?

Our story is about Hercules. No, not the mighty Greek God - but a pet hamster called Hercules. He isn't strong. He is a small, fluffy, lazy, hamstery slob.

How amazing, then, that Hercules is able to scare the townsfolk, crush cars and, trample the farmers' market in search of some delicious food.

How, you ask? Get a copy today and I'll tell you everything!

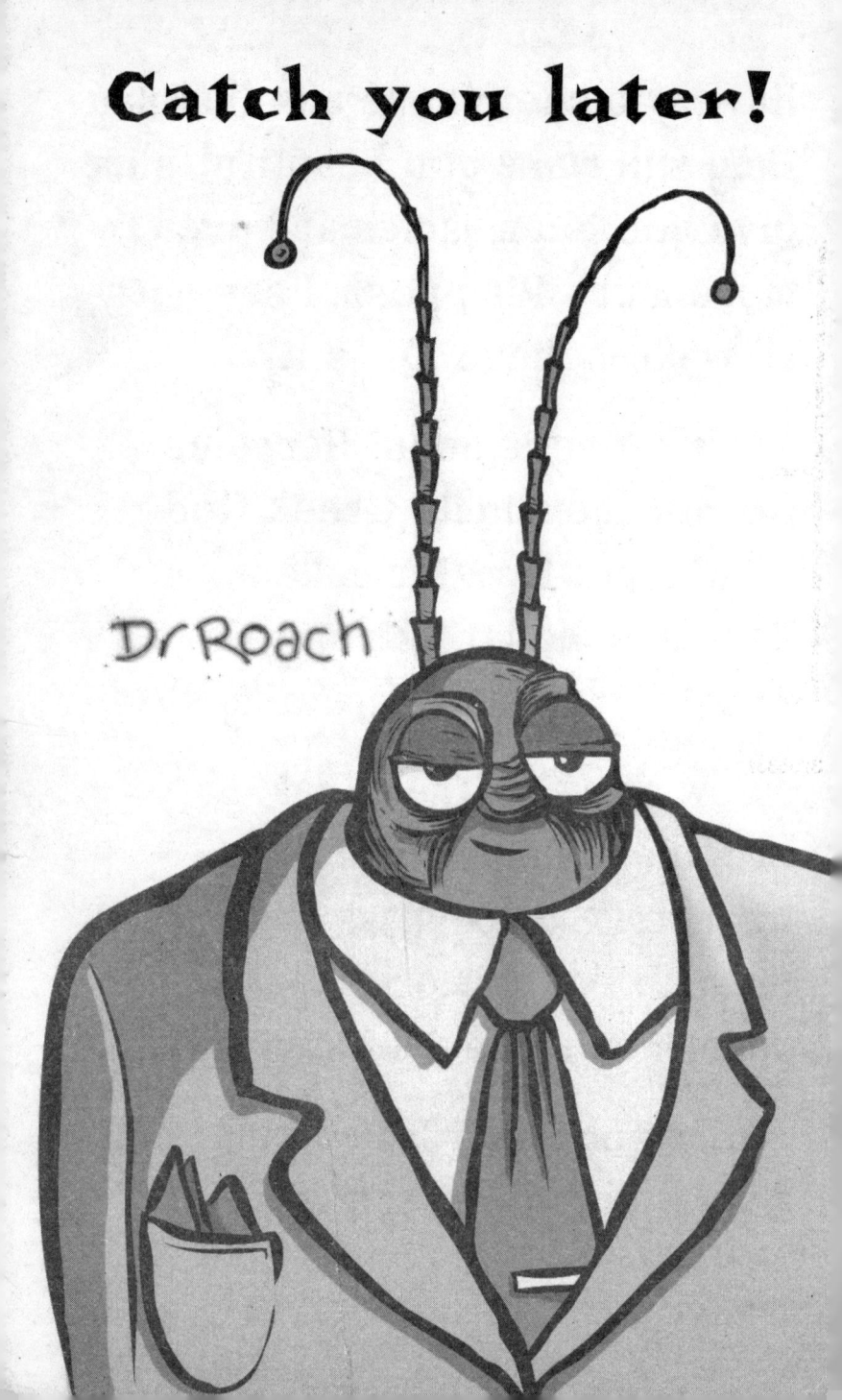